TIME RANGERS

1. A Shot in the Dark

Rob Childs

Hippo

DAZZA
GOALKEEPER — 1

WORM
RIGHT-BACK — 2

STOPPER
CENTRE-BACK — 5

RAKESH
RIGHT-MIDFIELD — 4

MR STOPPARD
MANAGER

JACKO
CENTRE-MIDFIELD — 8

SPEEDIE
RIGHT-WINGER — 7

RYAN
CENTRE-FORWARD — 9

ANIL
LEFT-WINGER — 11

MR THOMAS
MANAGER

For my wife Joy, with special thanks

Scholastic Children's Books,
Commonwealth House, 1–19 New Oxford Street,
London WC1A 1NU, UK
a division of Scholastic Ltd
London ~ New York ~ Toronto ~ Sydney ~ Auckland

First published in the UK by Scholastic Ltd, 1997

ISBN 0 590 13882 0

Typeset by DP Photosetting, Aylesbury, Bucks.
Printed by Cox & Wyman Ltd, Reading, Berks.

5 7 9 10 8 6 4

1 What does it mean?

"Shoot! C'mon, shoot!"

Rakesh hesitated a second longer, checking to see if someone else might be in a better position.

Ryan shouted again. "Don't take all day. Have a go!"

The chance was gone. His route to goal now blocked, Rakesh passed the ball to Jacko, his captain, instead. Jacko tried a hurried shot but the ball was charged down by a defender and the danger was cleared.

Ryan stood with hands on hips, giving a good impression of a simmering teapot. "What a waste!" he moaned. "No wonder you never score, Rakky. If that'd been me, we'd be two up now."

Rakesh didn't hang around to argue. He knew he should have had a pop at goal himself. He'd only scored one goal all season, and even that had been in his own net. He disappeared into midfield, hoping to win the ball back again for his team. That was the job he did best, not shooting.

"Leave off him, Ryan," the captain said. "Not everybody can score goals like you, remember."

Ryan shook his head. "You're not kidding. We'd have won the Double this season if some of the others had knocked a few in as well."

Jacko knew that was the main reason why Tanfield Rangers had only finished third in the Under-12 Sunday League. Lack of goals. Drawing too many games they should have won had cost them promotion. Thanks to Dazza's brilliance in goal, they'd managed to scrape a 1-0 victory in the Cup Final, but even Ryan's winner that day was from the penalty spot.

The Rangers were struggling to hold on to the same lead now. This first game of their Easter soccer tour of the Peak District was proving a tough one. They'd expected to walk it. The tour had been planned as a treat for the lads' hard work during the season, but they were having to work extra hard all over again to stay on top.

The home team of Oakbrooke St Stephen's had already tested Dazza's reflexes twice with firmly struck shots. When he was called into action once more, jumping high to snatch a curling cross out of the air, he waved his players away. "Out, defence, out!" he cried. "Leave them offside."

The visitors poured upfield, giving

Dazza multiple reminders of which team he was playing for. The name RANGERS was emblazoned proudly in white lettering across the backs of their smart, royal blue strip. The goalie hoofed the ball out to Anil on the left touchline and the winger set off on a long, loping run. His dribbling skills took him cleverly past two opponents and he still had time to look up and pick out his usual target.

There was Ryan, as always, demanding the ball at the far post. Anil's centre was hit a little behind the number nine but Ryan turned, chested the ball down and smacked it on the half-volley with his left foot. The ball soared high into the net beyond the Oakbrooke keeper's reach.

The captain was the first to catch Ryan at the end of the scorer's excited sprint of celebration. "Great goal!" Jacko screamed into his ear, dragging him to a

halt by his shoulders. "That's shown 'em!"

Ryan's first had only been a little gentle tap-in, so he was well pleased with this more spectacular second. "One more for my hat-trick," he grinned. "Another goal should clinch it for us."

His wish was not to come true. At the interval, he stood open-mouthed in disbelief as he found himself substituted. By his own dad, too, one of the team's joint managers.

"Why am I coming off?" Ryan complained, recovering from the shock.

"Don't be greedy, son," Mr Thomas said. "You've already got two goals, and we want to give somebody else a chance up front."

Mr Stoppard agreed. "We promised that all sixteen boys in the squad would play part of this first match, so we're making a number of changes for the second half. You're one of them, Ryan."

"Don't relax, lads, just because it's a friendly," said Mr Thomas after all the new positions had been sorted out. "Two-nil can be a dangerous lead. If you let the other team score, they're right back in the game."

The home side were not short of supporters. "C'mon, the Piggybacks!" shouted one of the parents. "You can still do it."

"Piggybacks!" Ryan snorted to the other players who had been replaced. "What kind of a nickname is that for a football team?"

Rakesh laughed. "It must be to do with that little logo they've all got on the front of their shirts. Like we've got T.R. on ours."

Ryan peered at the white shirt of the nearest Oakbrooke player who had turned round, annoyed at their giggling. "Weird. Looks like some kid giving another a piggyback ride."

"That's exactly what it is," the boy snapped back. "What's so funny about that? It's the symbol of our local church, Saint Stephen's."

Ryan shrugged. "So what's it supposed to mean?"

"It stands for helping other people."

"What, by giving them piggybacks? I've heard of a team carrying passengers, but that's ridiculous!" Ryan cackled. "I reckon your mates are gonna need more than piggybacks now to get out of this mess!"

2 Want any help?

The tourists could hardly have made a worse start to the second half.

Inside the first minute, the right full-back was caught daydreaming, gazing across the rooftops towards the tall spire of St Stephen's church.

"Watch out!" Dazza shrieked.

By the time Worm reacted, it was too late. The winger he was supposed to be marking had darted past him to slide the ball wide of the goalkeeper's desperate dive.

"Sorry," Worm murmured weakly. "Miles away."

"You should be!" muttered Dazza, fishing the ball out of the tangled netting. "What story were you thinking about then?"

Michael Winter wasn't called Worm for nothing. He was a good defender, at least normally, but off the pitch he was a real bookworm. In fact, he'd even once been caught trying to read a book during a match when the Rangers were well ahead and there was little to do in defence.

There was no time to settle down with a book now. Encouraged by the goal, Oakbrooke stormed back on the attack and kept Dazza as busy as he'd been all season. Jacko tried to rally his team to greater efforts but the many changes seemed to have upset the balance of the side. Some of the subs weren't quite sure just where they should be playing.

They paid the price at a corner-kick. The ball came over into the penalty area and centre-back Keith Stoppard found himself with two opponents to mark. Stopper, as he was known, failed for once to live up to his nickname. He chose the wrong boy, leaving the other free to nod the ball home from close range for the equalizer.

The Rangers party on the touchline hardly dared look for the rest of the game. Their own attacking moves were now almost non-existent but the Piggybacks seemed likely to score again at any moment.

"I've a nasty feeling we're going to throw this game away, if we're not careful," Stopper's dad sighed.

Mr Thomas nodded. "We did warn them," he remarked grumpily.

His own son recognized the danger too. "C'mon, Rangers!" cried Ryan. "Sort it out. We don't want to lose our first match of the tour."

Sadly, that's just what they did, with the next mistake coming from a most unlikely source – Dazza himself. Recently voted the club's "Player of the Season", despite all Ryan's goals, the keeper let the ball slip from his grasp as he sprawled across the goal-line. He had done well to save the original shot, but was helpless to prevent the striker blasting the loose ball into the net to put Oakbrooke ahead.

After another shot clanged against their crossbar and Stopper kicked a goalbound effort off the line, the Rangers were grateful to hear the final whistle and escape a bigger defeat.

"Lost three-two! Ridiculous!" Ryan fumed, making sure Dad could hear. "Would never have happened if I'd stayed on."

A Piggyback defender overheard him too, the same one that he'd ribbed at half-time. The boy tapped his logo and grinned at Ryan. "Any of your team want a lift back to the changing hut? They look a bit tired to me."

Ryan grunted but accepted that his joke had backfired on him. He shook hands to show there were no hard feelings. "Thanks for the offer, pal, but I think we'll manage somehow. Reckon you taught us a lesson today."

"Good teamwork, that's all it needs to help each other out of trouble," the boy smiled. "And I'm not just talking about football..."

Back in the two hired minibuses, the Rangers players consoled themselves by scoffing what remained of their chocolate eggs. It was still only Easter Sunday afternoon, but they had now already polished off the midnight feast planned for their first night under canvas.

"Right, lads, this is it!" cried Mr Thomas after a short journey.

"What?" mumbled Dazza through his last mouthful of chocolate.

"The campsite, of course."

"Where?" demanded Jacko, looking around for buildings. He needed two. A shop and the toilets. Not necessarily in that order.

"Here!" laughed Mr Thomas.

"But we're in the middle of an empty field," said the captain.

"Exactly!" Mr Thomas exclaimed. "Well away from civilization. You don't think we'd let you lot loose anywhere near other people, do you?"

"But there's nothing to do here, Dad," Ryan complained.

"I wouldn't say that," Worm butted in. "Oakbrooke's ancient monastery is in the next field, look. We can go and explore the ruins."

"Oh, brilliant!" Ryan groaned. "That's all we need. A pile of rotten old stones. I'm sure glad I'm not sharing a tent with you, Worm, if you're gonna drone on all night about its history."

"Not read anything about the place yet," he confessed. "But you can learn a lot from old ruins."

"Yeah," muttered Ryan. "I have to listen to one every day at school!"

Jacko laughed but then pointed towards part of the monastery site. "Wait a minute, it *could* prove useful to us."

"Don't you start getting like Worm."

"No, see those two stumpy pillars near that archway?"

"Yeah, what about them?"

Jacko grinned. "I thought you, more than anybody, might have noticed something about them. I reckon they're just about the right distance apart."

"What for?" Ryan asked, still not catching on.

"For a goal, stupid! Stick Dazza between them and we can get in some extra shooting practice while we're here."

"You certainly need it after that shocking performance this afternoon," said Mr Thomas as he clambered out of the driver's seat. "But first, it's all hands on deck to pitch camp."

Mr Stoppard, the driver of the second minibus, was already pulling the tent bags and other equipment off his vehicle. "Everybody out!" he shouted. "Come and grab some of this gear. We don't have any tea until we all help to make this field look like a five-star campsite!"

3 Where've they gone?

What followed was an hour of near chaos.

The boys had mixed success trying to erect their small, two-berth tents. Only those in the Tanfield Scouts Pack had any previous camping experience and theirs were the first to be set up.

"Ready!" cried Stopper. "What do we do now?"

"Well done," said his dad after inspecting the workmanship. "Your reward is to go and help some of the others get sorted out. Dazza and Rakesh are making a right pig's ear of things over there!"

Ryan claimed that he and Jacko had finished too, but his voice was muffled by the tent flap. They had decided to stay inside out of the way.

Mr Thomas came over to check, smiling. "Hmm, this is just a shot in the dark, lads, but I think that if I were to pull this rope you've left dangling down..."

"Don't do that! Aaghh!" Ryan's scream was cut off as the pair of them were buried under the collapsed canvas.

"Oh, dear!" Mr Thomas chuckled, enjoying the spectacle of two wriggling bumps trying to find the exit. "Guess what's happened?"

Ryan's ruffled mop of dark hair finally appeared. "Er, the tent fell down, Dad," he said sheepishly.

"Right, now do it again properly, you two, and don't be lazy this time. We're going to be here for two nights, remember."

Before moving on to play their next match in midweek, the boys had a busy programme of activities lined up. The two fathers planned to give them a long walk in the hills, visits to local places of interest and also a chance to watch the famous old Oakbrooke football game.

It was staged every year on Easter Monday as a tourist attraction to keep up an ancient custom dating back to the Middle Ages. For centuries, people would celebrate the festival by taking part in a rough and tumble ball game through the fields and lanes with the goals over a mile apart.

Worm was especially looking forward to that. He had read all about the history of football and wanted to see how the game might well have been played originally. But he couldn't wait for tomorrow. He was already off exploring by himself.

Mr Thomas looked around for more

victims. The toilet tents needed to be set up! "Anil, you and your partner go and fetch water from that standpipe at the edge of the field, please. Michael..."

He paused. "Where's Michael got to?"

"Dunno, Dad," Ryan said, banging one of the pegs firmly into the ground. "Not seen Worm since his tent was ready."

"I know where he's gone," Jacko began. "He's..."

Mr Thomas held up his hand for Jacko to stop. "Don't tell me, let me guess. He's wandered off to the old monastery, hasn't he?"

The boys round about grinned. "How did you know that?" Ryan piped up, hoping that Dad would take the bait on offer.

"Oh, just a shot in the dark," his dad sighed, automatically using his favourite expression.

The players fell about laughing. They

were well used to their manager coming out with that particular phrase when he wanted to make a sarcastic comment about something they'd been doing wrong in a game.

"What's the matter with you lot?" he asked, staring at them.

"Sorry, Dad, but that's the second time you've said that in the past five minutes. We're counting how many times it crops up during the tour."

Mr Thomas grinned to cover his embarrassment. "Cheeky monkeys! Right, if you've got nothing else better to do than that, there are still plenty of chores that need doing round here before it really does get dark..."

By the time Jacko led a group of players into the ruins for a kickabout before tea, there was still no sign of Worm.

"Wonder where he's nipped off to now?" Stopper grinned.

"Knowing Worm, he's probably slumped out of the wind behind a wall with a book for some peace and quiet," laughed Rakesh.

"Yeah, and to keep out of doing jobs, lucky thing," Ryan smirked. "Let's all go and find where he is and jump on top of him."

"Nah, leave him be," said the captain. "Let's get cracking with some practice now we're here. In goal, Dazza, go on."

Dazza hadn't even taken up his position between the broken pillars before Ryan belted their leather football at the target. The ball smacked into one of the stone bases and cannoned back past Dazza. It went straight to the feet of Rakesh who sidefooted the ball smoothly through the gap.

"Goal!" he yelped.

"Only 'cos I wasn't ready," said Dazza crossly.

"Why didn't you do that this afternoon, Rakky?" Ryan teased him.

Rakesh shrugged. "Didn't want to miss, I suppose."

"Everybody misses," Ryan said. "But if you don't shoot, you're never gonna score. You just have to keep trying."

Stopper and Anil opted to play as defenders, while Jacko, Rakesh and Ryan created shooting chances for each other by quick passes and good running off the ball into spaces. Dazza was in his element, delighting in throwing himself about in the long, springy grass.

The site of the ancient monastery was now neglected and rarely visited. Little remained of the place where a thriving community of monks once spent their lives in work and prayer. The building's foundations, a single small archway, a short stretch of crumbling wall and the stumps of a few thick pillars were all that had survived the ravages of time.

Jacko fooled Anil by shaping to pass the ball to Rakesh but chipped it instead over to Ryan, lurking free on the right. The striker caught it sweetly on the volley and the sheer power of the shot left Dazza groping at thin air. The ball sailed on, passing out of sight through the archway some distance behind.

"On your bike, Dazza!" Ryan chortled. "Go and fetch that beauty!"

Dazza slouched off, displaying the beaten goalie's familiar weary trudge to retrieve a ball that had no net to halt its progress. The others didn't even watch him go, sinking down into the grass to take a breather.

"Wonder if tea'll be ready soon?" said Anil.

"Hope so," replied Stopper. "I'm starving."

"Dazza's taking a long time," sighed Rakesh after a while. "What's he doing back there?"

"Probably looking in the wrong place," cackled Ryan, unable to resist a little boast. "He didn't even see the ball whizz past him."

"And he obviously still can't see it now," Jacko grinned.

"I'll go and help him find it," Rakesh said. "The grass must be even longer on the other side of that wall."

When Rakesh failed to return either, the others grew more impatient. "What are those two messing about at?" grumbled Stopper. "It can't have gone that far."

"C'mon, we'd better join in the search before Dad calls us for tea," Ryan said, scrambling to his feet.

As his friends disappeared through the archway one by one, Anil had a different idea. "I'll just go and find out what we're having," he said.

There was nobody about when Anil reported back to the ruins. Puzzled, he went to peer round the wall, expecting to see them all playing football in the field next to the monastery. It was empty, apart from a flock of sheep grazing beside a brook that snaked across the field towards the outskirts of the market town. He watched the antics of the newborn lambs for a few minutes then wandered slowly back to camp.

"Er, Mr Thomas," he began, "I know this is going to sound strange..."

"Nothing sounds strange any more after a season spent listening to all the crazy chatter of you lot," the manager said, turning the sausages in the pan for the last time. "I thought you were fetching the others back for tea."

"Yes, well, that's just it, you see," Anil frowned. "They've gone."

"Gone? What do you mean, gone?"

"They've all vanished," the boy said simply, before adding, "just like Worm..."

4 What's going on?

"Where have all these people suddenly come from?" Stopper gasped.

The three boys stood staring at a mass of muddy bodies scrummaging for something along the banks of a winding brook.

"It must be that old-style football game," said Jacko. "Funny, though, I thought that was on tomorrow."

"Perhaps it's a sort of practice," Ryan suggested.

"Looks real enough to me," Stopper said. 'They've all got dead old clothes on."

"Well, nobody's gonna wear their best

gear, are they, if they get all messed up like that," Ryan cackled. "Must be great fun!"

"There's Dazza and Rakesh!" cried Jacko. "That's why they didn't come back. They were too busy watching all this crazy stuff going on."

They ran over to join them near the brook. Dazza had their leather ball tucked under his arm.

"You could have told us what was happening," Ryan began to complain. "We thought you were still looking for the ball."

"We couldn't get back," Dazza stated flatly.

"Why not?" demanded Ryan.

"Take a look behind you."

The boys could not believe their eyes. Instead of the neglected ruins, there was a magnificent monastery, its tall, arched windows glinting in the rays of the setting sun.

Jacko shook his head and screwed his eyes tightly shut. But when he opened them again the monastery still stood there in all its graceful splendour. The wild cries and shrieks from the free-for-all around the brook echoed off its walls.

"Weird..." he breathed. "Nothing makes sense any more."

"What's going on here, Rakky?" Ryan hissed.

"No idea, but at least we've solved one mystery."

"What's that?" asked Stopper, still gawping at the building.

"Where Worm went to. Look, he's standing in the middle of the brook, screaming his head off."

Rakesh was right. As they watched, a dark object suddenly flew into Worm's arms and he waded desperately to the far bank to try and get out of the water. He never made it. A man launched himself down from the bank to push Worm

backwards and, as he toppled over, he was engulfed by other muddied bodies.

"C'mon, gang," Jacko yelled. "I think Worm's in some sort of trouble. He needs help."

Dazza hoofed their football into the air and whooped his way towards the crowded brook. By the time they reached Worm, however, the action had moved on. Worm was picking himself out of the shallow water, breathing heavily, but with the biggest grin they had ever seen.

"Worm!" cried Jacko. "Are you OK?"

"Hiya!" he laughed. "Sure. Wondered how long it would be before some of you also found that archway."

"What archway?" Ryan demanded.

"The one we all came through," Worm replied. "The one that must have transported us hundreds and hundreds of years back to the Middle Ages!"

"Don't talk stupid," Stopper told him.

"Just tell us what the heck is really going on here."

"I'm playing football."

"More like a riot from what we've seen."

"This is how it was centuries ago. Well, round about now actually."

"What do you mean, *now*?" Rakesh cut in. "I still don't understand."

Worm shrugged. "I can't explain it either, but we seem to have slipped back in time somehow."

Jacko pulled a face. "Come off it, Worm. That sort of thing only happens in stories, not in real life. The only time traveller I know of is Doctor Who!"

"You can't argue with the facts. Just look around you. Everything is different – how it used to be."

The others looked. Apart from the monastery, the market town of Oakbrooke across the fields was only a village, a smattering of small homes and farms. And there was no sign of any tents.

"C'mon, if this is all some sort of silly dream, we might as well have a bit of fun while it lasts!" cried Dazza. "Let's go and join in the game. Where're the goals?"

Worm grinned. "One of them is a packhorse bridge over the brook further on. Don't know about the other. We haven't got anywhere near it while I've been playing."

"Whose side are you on?" asked Stopper as he jogged along with the others towards the noise and the crowds.

"Whichever side's got the ball," laughed Worm.

"Isn't that against the rules?"

"There don't seem to be any rules. You just do what you want."

They caught up with the game again just as the ball was squirted out on to the bank right at Dazza's feet. Following his goalie's instincts, he was about to pick it up when he suddenly booted it away into the field for the mob to chase.

"What *is* that?" he cried in disgust. "It looks horrible."

"Probably a load of pigs' bladders all sewn up together," Worm answered. "I've read somewhere that's what they used in the past."

"Pigs' bladders! I'm not sure I want to play after all."

Dazza had no choice. The missile dropped back among them and they were quickly surrounded by other people, all trying to hack away at it at the same time.

"Reckon they need a few team tactics here!" Jacko panted, squeezing out of the crush. "They've got no positional sense."

"Talk about kick and rush. My dad would have a fit if he saw us playing like this," laughed Ryan.

Caught up in the excitement, they could not resist getting involved in the hurly-burly, non-stop action. Nobody seemed to take any particular notice of their appearance. The game attracted other strangers from outside the village and the boys' modern clothes of T-shirts, soccer tops and jeans were soon disguised by dirt and mud from the brook.

"Hey! They've got our ball!" cried Rakesh loudly. "They've started playing with it."

"Got to be better than their other one!" laughed Dazza. "Somebody obviously thought it was a good swap."

Jacko grinned. "I guess we've just gone and invented the leather football!"

And Rakesh was nearly the first player to score with one too! Standing near the narrow packhorse bridge, used by heavily-laden animals as they trekked across country along the ancient trade routes, the ball came to him unexpectedly. He didn't have time to think and dither. He simply hit it. The ball rocketed towards the target but was just too high, clipping the top of the bridge's stone parapet and bouncing over.

Rakesh received a mixture of cheers and jeers for his miss, with Ryan's voice among them. "Why didn't you pass to me?" he yelled, forgetting all about his earlier advice. "You'll never score from there."

"Don't listen to him, Rakky," said Jacko to encourage him. "You know what he's like. That was a great effort, the best yet."

The game continued to flow backwards and forwards through the rutted lanes and fields in the gathering gloom of the evening. The boys had all collected a few bruises and scratches, and when the ball was cleared over a hedge, they were glad to flop down for a rest at last.

"I'm just about done in," Worm wheezed. "Reckon I'm going to have a

look round the village for a spell. Can't miss a chance like this."

"This history lark's all very well for you," said Stopper, "but how are we going to get back to the future?"

"Maybe this witch's spell he's going to look for in the village will do the trick," Dazza grinned.

More seriously, they all looked towards Worm to provide the answer. He wasn't used to such attention and he considered his reply for a minute. "Well, the way I see it is this," he began as they listened eagerly. "We must have been brought back in time for a reason."

"What sort of reason?" asked Rakesh.

Worm sighed and stood up. "Who knows? That's what I'm hoping to try and find out. Perhaps then, we might be allowed to return – or be stuck here for good! Anybody coming with me?"

5 Who are you?

The village seemed deserted.

"They must all be out watching the game," said Stopper.

"Or playing in it," grinned Rakesh. "I saw a few old women trying to have a kick when the ball went near them."

Leaving the other three to rejoin the game, Stopper and Rakesh had followed Worm into the village until they reached the green. They had even dared to peep into a couple of empty cottages.

"This is incredible!" Worm enthused. "A real medieval village, and we've got it all to ourselves."

"I wouldn't quite say that," Stopper hissed, nudging him. "Look over there."

In the deepening darkness on the edge of the green slumped a small, ragged figure. Its feet were clamped in the stocks.

"He doesn't look any older than us," whispered Rakesh. "Wonder what he's done to deserve that?"

"Perhaps he scored an own goal!" giggled Stopper, but Worm silenced him with a glare.

"Let's go over and ask him and find out," he said.

"It's none of our business," Rakesh began to protest. "We don't want to go getting mixed up in anything. We're not even supposed to be here."

"Well, c'mon then," Worm urged, "before anybody gets back from the football and starts asking awkward questions."

They approached the wooden stocks

quietly, but the boy still jerked up straight. "I'm sorry," he whimpered. "I didn't mean to fall asleep..."

He stopped speaking and stared at them, uncertain what to make of these strangely dressed boys. "Who are you? Do you live here?"

Worm took the lead. "No, just visiting. Er, we're here for the game."

"Pray leave me alone," he answered. "You will get into trouble if you are seen talking to me."

"I told you," Rakesh warned, tugging at Worm's arm. "Let's get out of here while we can."

Worm pulled away. "What have you done?" he asked bluntly.

The boy shook his head, refusing to answer, but Worm persisted. "It must be bad to be put in the stocks on a day of celebration like this."

"It is. I was foolish."

"You ended up in there just for fooling

about?" gasped Stopper. "That's not right."

"He doesn't mean that, stupid," Worm muttered. "They didn't stick people in the stocks for nothing in those days."

"I stole two loaves of bread," came the mumbled confession.

"Is that all?" gasped Rakesh.

Worm looked stern. "You don't understand how serious this is, either of you. This kid could get himself hanged for stealing bread!"

They were both too shocked to reply, staring down at the young prisoner in pity and horror.

"What's your name?" asked Worm.

"Stephen."

"Right, Stephen, I'm Michael Winter and this is Stopper and Rakesh. We might be able to help you."

"Help him!" Rakesh spluttered. "Do you realize what you're saying, Worm? If this kid is in danger of getting hanged, we don't want to be seen as his mates."

Worm ignored him. "Why did you steal the bread, Stephen?"

"For my little brother, John. We do not come from these parts. We are travelling by ourselves, and he is lame. I have left him in a cave. He will be starving by now."

Stephen burst into racking sobs and Worm glanced round to check that no one else was nearby. "We've got to do something. We can't just leave him here. He must have been desperate for his brother to risk coming into a strange village to steal bread."

"Where are your parents?" asked Stopper. "Can they help?"

"They are both dead," Stephen sniffled. "We have nobody."

"Right, that settles it," Worm decided and strode over to pick up a rock from the bottom of a wall.

"What are you going to do with that?" asked Rakesh fearfully.

"We've got no time to go looking for the key to the lock so I'm going to try and smash the wood."

"What! People will be coming back any minute now. It's too dark to keep playing."

"Exactly. That's why we've got to act fast. You two get ready to help him on to his feet as soon as he's free. He's bound to be stiff after being trapped in this for ages."

They watched as Worm crashed the rock into the wood around the lock, splintering some of it away. But the wood was thicker and tougher than it looked.

"Built to last, these things," Worm panted. "Guess that's why you still see so many of them around today. I mean, in our own time."

He had several more goes, the noise

echoing alarmingly off the cottages around the green.

"C'mon, hurry up," Rakesh urged. "Or they'll be building more stocks – to put us in!"

Stopper lost patience and snatched the rock off Worm. "You're too weedy. Let me do it or we'll be here all night."

He tackled the wood the same way that he went in to opposing forwards – strongly and with great determination.

Suddenly, the wood cracked, and one more powerful blow split it enough for them to prise open the two halves of the stocks.

With help, Stephen was just able to drag his feet clear. His eyes were wide with panic, mirroring those of his would-be rescuers.

"Right, we've sure gone and done it now," gulped Rakesh. "What do we do next, clever dick?"

"We leg it fast," said Worm. "You two hold on to Stephen and I'll keep a watch out for anybody coming behind us."

"Which way, Stephen?" yelled Stopper. "Where's John hidden?"

Stephen pointed in the direction of the nearby hills, now lost to view in the darkness.

"Good, at least that's the opposite way to the football," said Worm. "Let's go. What are we waiting for?"

"What about the others?" cried Rakesh. "They won't know where we've gone."

"Nor will the villagers either. C'mon, there are lights heading this way. The game must be over."

"Wonder who won?" grunted Stopper as they headed for the hills.

"We have," muttered Worm under his breath. "With a bit of luck!"

6 Who scored?

"Time to switch on the floodlights, I reckon," grinned Jacko.

"How long does this game go on for?" asked Dazza.

"All night at this rate," replied Ryan, breathing heavily after chasing the ball across a field. "Or at least till somebody manages to score a goal."

"Nobody has scored yet, so far as I can gather," said Jacko.

"It's about time the others got back here as well," Dazza added. "I wonder what they're doing?"

"Knowing Worm, he's probably

sticking his nose in where he shouldn't," Ryan scoffed. "Especially if he's looking for that so-called reason why we're here."

By now, it was so dark, it was difficult to see the ball at all. But when it did come their way again, it looked different.

"Hey, our ball's been punctured!" cried Dazza.

"Huh, Dad won't be best pleased when we get back," snarled Ryan.

"*If* we get back..." Jacko corrected him.

The three boys once more plunged into the fray, forgetting for a while about their troubles. Jacko managed to get a couple of extra kicks of the burst ball in a scramble near the brook, and Dazza dived full length into the cold water to knock the ball further on towards the packhorse bridge.

This new attack was gaining ground rapidly and closing in on the goal.

Pressure of numbers was beginning to tell on the defenders protecting it. Some had dropped out of the game through injury or tiredness, allowing opponents to take up dangerous positions near the triple-arched bridge.

Ryan was one of them. His instinctive hunger for goals took him into a space on the gravel bank of the brook in front of the left-hand arch. The wider centre arch was the actual goal, still stoutly defended, but when the ball was hurled out of a frantic scramble, the Rangers' top scorer didn't hesitate.

Before anybody else could react, Ryan leapt up and met the floppy ball with a perfectly executed scissors-kick in mid-air. The speed of his acrobatics caught everyone by surprise. His right foot sent the ball looping past the defenders, and its wobbly flight deceived all of them. It clunked against the back of a man's head right underneath the bridge and

disappeared through the main arch for the first and only goal of the day.

It signalled the end of the game at last and the start of the night's festivities. Ryan found himself hoisted shoulder-high and the villagers began to form a procession behind him. Candles and wooden torches were lit and these burned brightly as the people cheered and jostled their way back towards the village. Jacko and Dazza had no option but to join in the celebrations, jogging among the procession as it wound along the lanes and on to the green.

Ryan had been given the battered football as his prize and he held it aloft in triumph as he sat unsteadily on his swaying perch, lapping up all the fuss. He was enjoying himself too much to notice the gradual change of mood of the crowd. His friends did. But the boys couldn't understand at first what had caused people to become angry when a few minutes ago they had seemed so full of fun and good spirits.

"What's going on?" asked Dazza as they managed to get together in the crush of bodies.

Jacko shrugged. "They're very upset about something. I'm not sure I like the look of this."

"Me neither. As soon as we can corner the great goalscorer by himself, I vote we try and slip away before anyone starts asking who we are and where we come from."

"Yeah, good idea. That last part might well prove a bit tricky!"

They discovered that a young thief had escaped from the stocks and a search of the village was being carried out. There was talk that he must have had some help from friends. The stocks had been smashed.

"Are you thinking what I'm thinking?" said Dazza.

"You don't reckon Worm would dare do something as crazy as that, do you?" Jacko replied.

They looked at each other and came to the same conclusion. "Right, where's Ryan?" said Dazza. "The sooner we get out of here, the better."

"That could be easier said than done," Jacko sighed, pointing Ryan out. "He's got completely carried away by all this business. Just look at him now, larking about like a loon with that group of kids around the maypole!"

"Psst!" a voice hissed from behind a low wall. "Over here!"

Jacko peered into the darkness. "Who's there?"

"Worm! We're all in danger. No time to explain. We've got to leave."

"That's just what we'd decided. The people are hopping mad about what's happened."

"Didn't think they'd be amused. Where are the others?"

"Dazza's trying to get hold of Ryan. He scored the winning goal and he's the big hero round here tonight."

"Well, he won't be by morning. We've all got to escape while it's still dark."

It took another five minutes to drag Ryan away from the green and into the shadows. "What's all the rush?" he complained. "I've left the ball some-where back there."

"Doesn't matter about that now, it's time to go," said Jacko.

Worm urged them to follow him. He put a finger to his lips to signal everyone to keep quiet, but Ryan was too hyped up to obey. "Hey! What is all this? Why are we sneaking away? It's like I'm being kidnapped."

Worm amazed the others and even himself by going up to Ryan and stand-ing directly in front of him, face to face.

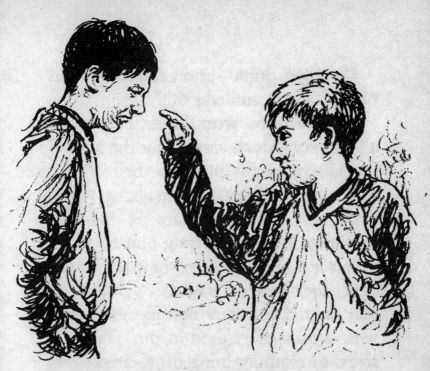

"For once, just shut up, will you, and do as you're told."

Normally, Worm would not have dared to say anything like that to Ryan, but it seemed to work. Ryan was speechless. They crept out of the village, left the lane and ventured across a field. As they neared the brook, four figures emerged from their hiding-place among the bushes.

"Stephen, John – meet the rest of our gang," Worm smiled grimly.

Introductions were brief. They were all still very much afraid that the men of the village might pick up their tracks, even at night. The new arrivals, however, could not help but stare at the two brothers, John supporting himself shakily on a rough staff. In the pale moonlight, they were a pathetic sight, black hair matted and their thin faces streaked with weeks of ground-in dirt. Tattered strips of clothing hung off their skeletal bodies, and the eyes of the players were drawn like moths to a flame to little John's left leg which finished at the ankle.

To the bewildered brothers themselves, all these well-built, well-fed boys who spoke so strangely seemed almost like young gods. Stephen put his arm protectively around John's shoulders, steadying him, and addressed them as bravely as he could. "Thank you for rescuing us. We owe our lives to you," he began, his croaky voice becoming more firm as he continued. "I do not know where you come from, but you must leave us now and go your own way. It is too dangerous for you to stay with us. We will slow you down."

They all knew that what Stephen said made good sense, but none of them wanted openly to agree with him. They hated the idea of having to abandon the brothers now. Worm brushed Stephen's concerns aside.

"We're teammates, you and us. We stick together," he said. "C'mon, everybody, we need to get further away from the village."

As they started off again, Stephen lifted John up on to his back to travel more quickly.

"Can we help?" asked Jacko. "We could take it in turns to carry him."

"We've already offered," said Stopper. "He refuses. He carried John all the way down the hillside like that."

"He's not heavy," Stephen grunted. "He's my brother."

7 Can we come in?

Rakesh held up a black, misshapen object. "Look what we found in the field before you got here," he chuckled quietly. "The old ball."

"Can I have it as a souvenir?" Ryan begged, then glanced at Worm accusingly. "I had to leave ours behind in all the panic."

"Give it to him, Rakky, or we'll never hear the last of it," said Worm.

The boys spoke in hushed tones as they followed the course of the brook, swapping news with each other about events since they split up. Ryan bragged of his goal and Worm described how they had managed to locate the small cave in the hills to reunite the two brothers.

"So what are we going to do now?" Stopper demanded to know.

They all looked expectantly towards Worm. He was the only one who appeared to have any kind of plan and had assumed the role of leader quite naturally. "We're going up to the monastery," he said simply.

"The monastery! Why?" asked Jacko.

"Because it's the safest place there is round here. The villagers will be searching everywhere for us tomorrow, but in the olden days you could go to a church or monastery like this and ask for sanctuary."

"What's that?" interrupted Dazza.

"It means somewhere you can't be captured and punished," Worm explained. "They won't be able to touch us once we're in there, even if they find out where we are."

"What do we do? Just go up and knock on the door and say please, can we come in?" Ryan sneered.

Worm nodded. "Yeah, something like that. Got any better ideas?"

Ryan shrugged. "Only to get back home to the campsite."

"OK, this is where we first came in, isn't it, the monastery?" said Worm. "So maybe this is the way we might get back again as well."

"Shut up!" hissed Stopper. "Listen!"

Raised voices drifted to them on the wind. "They're after us!" cried Rakesh. "They're on our trail."

Fear gripped them. This was no game of hide and seek. They knew this was for real – a matter of life or death!

"C'mon, let's keep moving, fast as we can," Worm urged. "It's not far to the monastery now."

"You bomb on ahead with Rakesh," Jacko told him. "Go and pound on that door like crazy so they'll be ready to let us in when we get there."

Worm hesitated, reluctant to leave them, until Dazza pushed him forward. "Go on, quick, both of you. The men are still some way back by the sound of it. We'll be OK."

As Worm and Rakesh disappeared into the night, splashing across the brook, the others assessed their chances. "The villagers won't know exactly where we are yet," Stopper said, as much to try and reassure himself as anybody.

"No, but I bet they've guessed where we might be going," Jacko replied, swallowing hard. "They'll be making straight for the monastery, hoping to head us off."

"Right, we've got to make sure we get there first, then," Ryan stressed and suddenly snatched John off his brother's back and hauled him up on to his own. Stephen immediately began to protest, but Ryan cut him short.

"No arguing, mate," he said fiercely. "I'm bigger and stronger than you. This is the survival of the fittest. You follow close to me. C'mon, run!"

They ran. The race was on. After fording the brook, they could now clearly hear the chasers somewhere behind them, their shouts louder than ever. But the boys were also able to make out the silhouette of the monastery buildings against the night sky and this spurred them on, lungs bursting, to even greater efforts.

It wasn't long before Worm and Rakesh were hammering their fists on the wooden front gate of the monastery. Even then, they suffered an agonizing wait before anybody responded. Bolts rattled back, the gate creaked ajar and a monk in a brown habit appeared in the opening, his face hidden from view by the deep folds of the hood. After a brief, whispered exchange, Worm was ushered inside.

"Stay there and keep a lookout for the others," he told Rakesh. "I'll be back, promise."

"What'll we do if the men get here in the meantime?" Rakesh asked desperately.

It was too late. Worm was gone and the gate closed. "Just don't invite them in for supper, I guess," Rakesh muttered to himself, clinging on to the shreds of his sense of humour for comfort. He kept expecting hordes of angry villagers to leap out of the darkness at any minute and when he saw scurrying shadows coming towards him, he crouched down, heart in his mouth.

"Jacko!" he gasped aloud in recognition. "Am I glad to see it's you!"

"The men are right behind us!" Jacko panted as he was joined by the rest of the group with Stopper bringing up the rear. "Where's Worm?"

The gate reopened at that very moment and Worm waved them all through urgently. Only just in time. As he peeped out before slamming the stout gate and helping the monk to slide the metal bolts across into position again, he spotted a number of figures charging over the field towards them.

Stephen lifted his brother to the ground and gave him his short staff while Ryan bent forward, hands on knees, to recover his breath.

"Thank you," a little voice piped in his ear. It was the first time Ryan had heard John make a sound.

"Any time, John," he wheezed, forcing a smile as he saw the boy's face, white with terror under the dirt. Ryan straightened up and winked at Stephen, remembering what the Oakbrooke player had said to him. "Any time big brother can't give you a piggyback, you just come to me. It's all about good teamwork, eh?"

The monk escorted them quickly into the main building away from the noise beyond the perimeter walls. He removed his hood, revealing a round, shaven tonsure on the top of his head and a warm smile of welcome underneath. "I am Brother Dominic," he said as he showed them to a large room, lit only by a few shimmering candles. "Please eat."

The boys sat down at a long oak table where bread, cheese and water were brought to them by two more monks, almost identical in appearance. Few words were spoken. The footballers had forgotten how hungry they were and the young brothers hadn't seen food for days. Everybody was too busy eating to speak until they were once more left on their own.

"I've told Brother Dominic about the business with the stocks," Worm began, chewing on a crust.

"So what will they do with us?" asked Jacko.

"We'll have a bed for the night at least. They never turn anybody away. They always give food and hospitality to strangers who come seeking shelter."

"And what about after that?" Stopper persisted. "What's going to happen to Stephen and John – and the rest of us for that matter?"

Worm glanced across the table at the brothers. John was already nearly falling asleep, his mouth still crammed with cheese. "I don't know for certain. We've got to go and see the big boss man, the abbot, in the morning to tell him how we arrived here."

"That's going to be interesting," muttered Ryan.

"Hmm ... we'll have to see if we can come up with some believable story," said Jacko. "Will the brothers be OK, do you think?"

Worm nodded. "Don't see why not. The monks won't hand over a couple of kids to the village mob, whatever they may have done. They'll find protection here until the whole thing blows over. Then I guess they might be able to choose whether to stay or go on their way."

Stephen had been trying, with difficulty, to follow their conversation and now joined in. "Do not worry about us. You have already done more than enough to help us. I like it here. It feels ... peaceful."

Worm looked thoughtful. "Did you say you have no home to go to, Stephen?"

He shook his head sadly. "No home. We do not even know our family's name. I am sorry, Michael, I cannot remember yours. Do your friends call you W ... Worm?"

The others laughed as Worm flushed. "It's Winter, Michael Winter," he answered.

"Winter," Stephen repeated. "Yes, that is a fine strong name."

Brother Dominic returned before

Worm was embarrassed further. "We have prepared your bedding. This way, please."

The monk led the boys along dimly lit passages, past the cloisters, before pausing by a small archway. "I shall take Master Stephen and Master John to a private, separate part of the building where they will be safe," he explained. "The rest of you can sleep together in our guest room through this door. Good night."

"Our thanks, Brother Dominic," Worm said formally. "We are all very grateful for everything that you have done."

The monk bowed his head slightly as Stephen stepped forward. "Forgive me," he said to his rescuers, "but I sense somehow that we may not see each other again. I know you must have to go on a long journey. We shall never forget you..."

"Thank you," John murmured shyly again and they all laughed.

The boys watched as the three of them went off down the passage. The monk, holding a lantern, shuffled along in his sandals while little John tried to keep up, hobbling on his staff. Stephen, barefoot, walked slowly at his brother's side and half-turned to wave goodbye.

Rakesh yawned and stretched. "I'm too tired to go on any long journey. What did he mean by that, I wonder?"

8 How do you know that?

One by one, the footballers filed sleepily through the archway, emerging under a clear, starlit sky. They stood in a bewildered group, blinking at the eerie ruins around them and trying to make sense of where they were.

They looked behind them at the only surviving arch of the monastery. "It must once have been the door into the guest room!" gasped Stopper.

"And now it's brought us back to our own time!" cried Dazza.

Ryan took in great gulps of the cold night air. "I never thought I'd be so pleased to see this old place again," he sighed with relief.

"There's the fire in the middle of the campsite," said Jacko. "They must all have been going frantic. What's the time?"

"Midnight!" answered Rakesh. "We've been lost for hours."

Only Worm didn't join in the babble. He gazed at the archway wistfully and moved towards it. "And where do you think you're going?" Jacko said firmly, stopping him short.

"Er, I just thought I'd go back and check..."

"Don't you dare. We're not going through there again – ever!"

Their sudden reappearance in the camp startled everybody. All the other boys were still up, huddled in sleeping bags around the fire while the two dads were talking to policemen. They stared as the six missing players strolled back into camp from the ruins, their faces filthy and their clothes torn and caked in dried mud.

For a moment, nobody spoke. Then they were engulfed by children and adults alike, hugging and scolding them at the same time, all wanting to know where they'd been.

"We've been crazy with worry, helping the police search for you," cried Mr Stoppard. "But look at the state you're in!"

"And what on earth's that disgusting thing?" Mr Thomas demanded.

Ryan realized he was still holding the old pigs' bladder ball. "Um..." he began and then hesitated as Jacko whispered into his ear.

"Don't even bother trying to explain. They'll never believe us!"

The boys spent a short, restless night in their tents.

What little sleep they had was haunted
by strange dreams. Rakesh saw himself
locked in the stocks, while Stopper
relived their desperate search to find
John, half-starved, in a bare, freezing
cave.

Jacko's and Dazza's personal night-
mares were sparked off by that terrify-
ing chase across the fields to the
monastery, which seemed to float in the
shadows ever further away from them.
Only Ryan dreamt of the football game
itself. His sleep was disturbed by images
of mud and water, by his glorious goal
and the torchlit procession into the
village. He woke up at one point,
convinced the whole thing had been just
a dream – until he reached down and
put his hand on the pigs' bladder ball by
his side.

And Worm? Michael Winter scarcely
slept at all. His mind was too full of
everything he had seen and done during

their incredible adventure in a bygone age. He'd even stood up to Ryan and earned new respect. He doubted whether the others would make fun again of his love of history.

As dawn broke, he switched on his torch to read the guidebook of Oakbrooke he had borrowed from Mr Thomas. He hadn't yet had a chance to look at it and now his eye was suddenly caught by a mention of his own surname. Breathlessly, he read the caption underneath a photograph of an ancient tomb in the chancel of St Stephen's church.

"...*the final resting place of the greatest abbot the local monastery had ever known. Because of its importance, the tomb had been moved into the church when the monastery was destroyed in the sixteenth century, after which the church was re-dedicated to honour the town's patron saint.*"

Worm could not contain his excitement. Trampling on his partner in his haste, he scrambled out of the tent, barefoot in the wet grass and still in his pyjamas, to stare at the ruined monastery in the early morning mist. He tried to picture in his mind's eye the wonderful building as it had once been centuries ago – how he had actually seen it the day before.

The boys had an appointment later that morning at the police station. Their story about wandering too far away, getting lost and falling into the brook hadn't sounded very convincing the night before, and would probably be even less so in the cold light of day. But they decided to stick to it as being rather more believable than the truth.

As the squad of players walked into Oakbrooke, the two dads tried to give them a potted history of the market town from the guidebook. But all the six time travellers wanted to see was the inside of St Stephen's church. Worm had enthused about his discovery over breakfast, but without giving too much away. He wanted to enjoy their surprise.

"Good to see you taking such an interest in churches suddenly," said Mr Stoppard as he led them in, but found he was talking to himself. The lads had dashed past him straight up the nave into the chancel.

"There! Told you!" cried Worm triumphantly as they stood, lost in thought, gazing at the large table tomb in front of them. On top of it was a memorial brass, life-size, showing two robed, hooded figures side by side, their hands together in prayer. What mesmerized the boys, however, was that one of the men had his left foot missing.

"Saint Stephen!" Worm announced. "Or Father Stephen Winter, as he was known, before they made him into a saint after his death."

"Could just be a coincidence," murmured Rakesh without conviction.

"It can't be our Stephen, surely," said Stopper, shaking his head. "He was just a scraggy little kid who was caught stealing a couple of loaves of bread. If we hadn't released him, he might even have been hanged."

"Right, but remember him asking me about my surname during the meal? The brothers didn't have one of their own. They must have decided to use mine when they wanted to start a new life at the monastery," Worm jabbered on proudly. "Just look what the inscription says on the tomb."

"I'm trying to," said Jacko, "but it's all in some funny language."

"Latin," Worm told him and read the translation from the guidebook. *"Stephen and his brother John, a cripple, performed great deeds of charity. They devoted their lives to helping poor and sick children after being saved from death as orphans themselves by mysterious young strangers...*"

"Wow! That must mean us!" Dazza whooped.

Jacko had managed to work out the dates on the tomb. "They both died in the same year. Exactly six hundred years ago!"

Ryan let out a low whistle. "Hey! One of the carvings on the side of the tomb shows a little kid being given a piggy-back!"

"I was just coming to that," said Worm, irritated that Ryan had seen it first. "It became their kind of trademark, I suppose. It's engraved on each corner of the brass, too, look."

"A bit like a Saint Christopher's medal," Stopper put in.

"It's the same design as those Oak-brooke players had on their shirts,"

Rakesh said. "Their defender said it stood for helping other people."

"So that's obviously what the brothers must have done all their lives," Worm finished. "Amazing how things can work out sometimes, isn't it?"

"With a little help from your friends," chuckled Rakesh.

Back outside again, the lads noticed a set of old stocks, erected in the church-yard for visitors to examine. Worm didn't need the guidebook to confirm that they were genuine. He caught Stopper's eye and knew that his partner-in-crime had also recognized the tell-tale crack in the upper part of the wooden frame.

Everywhere in the town there were posters advertising the big football game taking place that afternoon. "Huh! Anyone welcome to join in, they say," scoffed Jacko. "Bet it's nothing like the *real* thing!"

"Should still be good fun, though," said Dazza. "Shall we have a go?"

"Might do," grinned Ryan. "If they need somebody who can score!"

His dad stopped them briefly at the main road bridge. "One of their goals has always been on this spot, apparently," he said, quoting from the book. "You can still see some ancient stonework underneath the modern bridge. Anybody got any idea what used to be here long ago?"

Ryan glanced round at the others and raised his hand. "Er, perhaps an old packhorse bridge, Dad?"

Mr Thomas looked at his son in astonishment. Ryan was not exactly noted for his knowledge of history, unless it was remembering the final team placings in last season's league tables. "Dead right. How on earth do you know that?"

Ryan giggled, unable to resist the

temptation. "Oh, just a shot in the dark, Dad, you might say!"

The time tour continues with Time Rangers 2.
A Blast from the Past

"C'mon, Rangers!" urged their captain. "Let's show 'em we mean business."

Jacko led by example as usual. His sleeves rolled up, he crunched into his next tackle in midfield, winning the ball cleanly and playing it forward to Ryan. "Go for goal!" he yelled.

Rangers' leading scorer never needed any such encouragement. By instinct, he turned with the ball to create a shooting angle for himself outside the Braves' penalty area but was crudely upended by his marker.

Ryan jumped to his feet and glared at the big defender. "Dirty foul, that. Back off, will you, and keep the plague to yourself!"